Triple No. 13

Deborah Woodard
Robert McNamara
Erin M. Bertram

The Ravenna Triple Series
*Chapbooks as they were meant to be read—
in good company.*

*This project was supported in part by a
Creative Arts Grant from the City of Edmonds*

COPYRIGHT © Ravenna Press, 2020
All rights reserved, reverting on publication to the individual authors

ISBN: 978-1-7351131-4-2

Published by Ravenna Press
USA
ravennapress.com

FIRST EDITION

Mill Girls
  by Deborah Woodard   *page* 1

To Hell and Back
     &
My SARS-CoV-2, Thus Far
  by Robert McNamara   *page* 39

Gender/Genre
  by Erin M. Bertram   *page* 73

Acknowledgments & Biographies

Deborah Woodard

Mill Girls

Author's Note

Mill Girls is a collaged, compressed, and augmented retelling of Lucy Larcom's now-forgotten, book-length narrative poem in blank verse, *An Idyl of Work* (1875). In *Idyl*, Larcom left us a unique work, an epic of women's labor, learning, and friendships. Larcom tells the story of Lowell, Massachusetts's mill girls and the New England textile industry. In this early chapter of antebellum factory work in the United States, a native-born pool of young women from small New England farming communities were employed by the new textile mills, lived in closely supervised boarding houses, and, albeit in a paternalistic gesture of benevolence, were encouraged to attend classes and lectures and even to publish their creative efforts in the company-sanctioned literary journal, *The Offering*. My goal in *Mill Girls* was to extract the thematic core of *An Idyl of Work*, while retaining the narrative (minus blank verse) in an abbreviated form. Additionally, I collaged, and at times combined, the interspersed songs and ballads. Could I, in effect, collaborate with Lucy Larcom in retelling this chapter of American textile labor? *Mill Girls* is still settling with me, but I feel that the answer is yes.

Contents

Overture: Spring Song for Many Voices 5
The Mill 7
Hiking and Reading 14
Cousin Zillah Wray 16
Girl Sabbath 18
Clouds on Whiteface 21
Elinor Salutes Whiteface 24
Prelude to a Ballad 25
The Ballad of Peggy Bligh 27
Ralph and Elinor 31
Lost Girl Bella 32
Bella's Song: When Wings are Gone 35
Encore: Pathos of the City Lights 37

Overture: Spring Song for Many Voices

*Blushing into bloom with lightness,
apple blossoms budding, blowing*

*are here to thorn us
in the soft May air.*

*We need the heart of spring,
heralds of goodwill*

*from the happy trees!
What shall we do? Love is dreaming*

*in dappled lanes.
Words are more than idle seeming—*

*Cramped and stilted from winter still,
but showering petals everywhere:*

*over boarding house and mill,
boughs flush into bloom—*

*Why are we gowned unequally?
O, to wear such rose-touched whiteness!*

*Flakes of fragrance—drifting, snowing.
Cups with sunlight overflowing*

*through to ripe fruit's taste,
gentle souls into love-light blushing.*

*Tongues to utterance rushing—
fairy promises, out gushing—*

*the apple petals falling—
gay scarf and veil and parasol laid aside.*

*What can we, ashamed of girlish scheming,
give straightaway to life?*

The Mill

Some strangers came one day into the mill. Saw

    I was so glad to hear from you again. *

arms, hands, and heads move with the moving

    Is it babyish? I wish I could feel your arms

looms. A hundred girls who hurried to and fro

    about me, and one of your well-remembered

click-clacked the shuttles.

    kisses on my lips.

Hid within the earthquake were

    I had my dress cut yesterday.

rumbling and mingled smells, pitched voices

    I tried it on last night and it set beautifully.

making music. Lithe forms spanned wide

> *I am having it made with a deep*

webs, or stooped, tho comely—so the visitors

> *yoke in it and pleated and a belt.*

wondered, pitied; smiled perhaps.

> *They have a great many cut so now.*

Bobbin changers in pinafores shared

> *Aurelia has red hair that curls all 'round*

one motion. For the most part tidy,

> *her head, and looks sweetly I will tell you.*

their eyes glowed like mysterious wheels,

> *She's like a kitten that is just a-getting its eyes open.*

made emphasis for themselves.

> *I believe you have heard about such ones before.*

When the lunch bell rang, noses plunged

> *Mother has been in to see the Candy*

into pinks and honeysuckle outside the gate.

> *Man again and got more than she*

With time and noise enough, the strangers

> *can eat in a week. Says she would send you*

disappeared like key into a lock.

> *a good piece in a letter if she could.*

Gossamer motes of Elinor's plants:

> *Seeing such a sight of*

roses, and one great oleander

> *pretty things, it makes me*

blooming against the panes, intensified.

> *want to get rich right away.*

The strangers peered with curious eyes

> *Last night I put thirty dollars in*

into the carding room. Sunbeams thickened

> *the Appleton Bank. Mr. Winnek*

into golden bars across uneven boards.

> *is very kind and pleasant.*

Elinor and Bella worked side by side

> *I had a letter from home a short time since,*

in a sunlit corner that looked out

> *and Father is having the blues for the grasshoppers*

on the furrowed river.

> *are eating everything and he hasn't got any horse.*

Elinor's thoughts turned to seeking clews.

Horses were handsome, their manes

She resumed work in silence; not unmissed

braided with flowers.

by the good Superintendent, a grave man,

A balloon went up with one man in it:

who held a covetous glint, a close, cold mouth.

I had an altitudatiously good time!

Hands and eyes followed the shuttle's flight,

We shall have looms together. Aurelia is

to disentangle, or comb

a dear sweet girl, haven't I been smart?

untrimmed cloth, there lingering.

We went to another cotillion party.

But work's a blessed curse, and temples throb

> *I have commenced another class.*

among swift belts and pulleys

> *I did not whisper last term, and I am not going*

the spindles buzzing like a thousand bees.

> *to whisper this term, if I can help it.*

Now sir, this should not be.

> *I have also been to meeting this Sunday.*

When a child toils in close air like this,

> *A grand meeting & grand Singing.*

a bobbin-star amid the cloudlike nebulae,

> *I think that your journey here*

you're copying our British faults too closely.

> *must have been most arduous.*

Bending over her work again,

> *Dorrit sent me a present of a Gold ring.*

Elinor cracked open a little book

> *Very kind of her I must say!*

beneath a warp-fringe from her loom.

> *I will write an immediate answer*

The Superintendent winked: she is continually

> *and enclose a pair of Stockings.*

anxious for more work. She can do it, too.

* The italicized lines of dialogue are excerpted from the Lowell mill girl letters of Anonymous, Emma Lizzy Clough, and Addie Holmes.

Hiking and Reading

I shall read my Wordsworth better now,
said Elinor, not the least his long *Excursion*.
It has its flowerless, barren stretches, like any
solitary mountain road, but along the way
echoes from deep forests welcome us.

At work, offered Minta, a line of poetry
is such a lift from the monotonous clatter:
an airy tidbit from Shelley's "Skylark"
evokes for me the south wind's tenderness.

They looked down to the river.
Streams they loved were busy.
No bleak mountain path but unveiled
surprise of fragrant thicket where crickets
mimicked the din of looms:

>   *Toil is warp and money weft.*
>   *Merry days go dancing by,*
>   *turning mill folks dizzy.*
>   *Air is warp, and sun is weft.*
>   *They heal the pale-faced girls.*
>
>   *Along green-fringed canals,*
>   *hard work comes and tarries.*

Children, we'll be fairies
such as haunt old stories.

Never would Elinor and Minta spend a day
of sunlit peak, of crag and page for naught.

Life is warp, and love is weft,
hid in morning glories.

They possessed power of strange withdrawal
into heaven, such blooms obtained.

Cousin Zillah Wray

Ambrose, my intended, met my cousin
somewhere on the road,
said Ruth at last—sweet Zillah Wray.

You see, he I loved—and love still, with a
difference—
had gone part way upon his journey, sending
words of newly constrained tenderness to me.

Though crushed, I was not wholly unprepared,
for I remembered Zillah. Ah, Juggernaut
experience never heeds its victim's cry!
I should scorn the man pretty faces could enslave!

Like a Sabbath dress,
fetching, and so kept in wearing trim,
was her unconscious show of artlessness.

Yet Zillah loves. Perhaps I do her wrong.

Mine was the penalty of reticence.
Foolish Cordelia should have answered Lear.
Fondness, I believed, was treasure men should seek,
and, being hid, prize all the more. It is not so!
The branch cloven and brought low.

Perhaps, offered Elinor, your Ambrose is smitten
solely with himself, glassed in her admiration.

> Tis fancy's glimmer, on both sides,
> never love.

Yes, Ruth said. Oh, I can hear just how Zillah
put it, as she strolled with Ambrose.
Bewitching as true dawn or mountain brooks,
she spoke of me.

> She rounded her lips so prettily
> Ambrose sighed to kiss them.

Her guilelessness seemed natural as life itself.
Sure, this rose is beautiful, but only for a day or two.
Try as I will, the thought of him comes back to me:

> He's usually in shirtsleeves.
> He seems to need me, as I needed him.

> Yet who is not her own mistress?
> Thereupon, I came to Lowell
> full of Eden-visions about mills.

With him, I loved a sealed-up sepulcher.
Ambrose is not mine or she could not have won him.
Still, the wheel grinds on, the red drops ooze…

Girl Sabbath

Together walked
under May's fragrant sunshine:
Elinor, Minta and Bella; Emmeline, Ruth,
and Sarah, as Sabbath sun
shawled them up the windy slope.

Girl Baptists, Girl Universalists, Girl Methodists,
Girl Unitarians and Girl Orthodox
sweetly attired, next maidens Quaker-prim.

All filled brick-paven streets and sandy paths
with brows demure.
                              With gingham gowns,
straw bonnets, and smooth, parted hair.

--

That Sabbath in the air
which made New England as old Palestine—
Every leaf of every tree whispered
some parable or reverent tale.

Sabbath for lives unwound from labor's coil.
Sabbath rest among the weary wheels
that ceased their groaning with a conscious hush.

--

Enough! laughed Minta. *I'll hold my tongue
about the stiff-necked, strait-laced Orthodox.
The hard, cold way of prayer those stern men chose.*

*It was like a toilsome journey 'round the world,
by Cathay and the mountains of the moon.*

I swear I'd rather be a Patagonian.

Well, pressed Elinor, *but at Saint Ann's
nobody vexed you?*

*No, the ups and downs just suit my restlessness.
The prayer-book place, that bothers me, though.*

--

The sweet, old-fashioned day had left them now
with unblinking thoughts that stumbled sometimes,
awkward with strange consciousness,
through lattice-work of apple boughs
                    shirring diamond shadows.

Could the breeze have wandered with so
delicate a breath through the garden of the famed
Hesperides?

Minta knew all the birds owned the sky,
the glory of new Jerusalem,
an olivet of every green ascent.

Elinor settled herself against the sofa's arm
in listening posture, and Emmeline
cried eagerly, *Do!* And Minta replied:

Now I shall read what I have written.

Clouds on Whiteface

'Tis curious, said Elinor, *the naming of these hills.*

Her eye rested upon Black Mountain's top
of somber velvet, highest of the peaks.

But he's less grand than Whiteface, his next-neighbor,
peering sharp-cut and gray out of the north,
with outreach of bare shoulder.

>   Perched on fern-wreathed rocks, Elinor, Minta,
>   Ruth, and Bella saw
>   through veils of rain,
>   green summits come and go:

>   a mountain's purple slope, with unadulterated
>   color out to the northern sky, from east
>   to west, then that bright cone of perfect emerald

>   where trout streams
>   flowed through birchen intervals.

Were Whiteface sorcerer or not, Elinor resumed,
he's a cloud-compeller still, whose head,
worn and haggard from the storms
pours clearest oil and wine.

*Here's a picture of him, from the same
stray rhymer's pencil, showing possible moods.*

--

The girls stayed on an evening and a morning
in a cabin by the lake. The summer seemed to go
by floating, a chain of ever-varying pearls.

Elinor sat still, as one entranced, her dove-like
eyes filled with unutterable light. Minta stood
in her cottage bonnet and bright shawl
set to companion restless Bella.

It was an idyl of work, as work fell idle.

Back to the music of the spinning wheel, said Ruth,
to clothe ourselves at hand looms of our own,
as did our grandmothers. The loom for eons
held its humble symmetry.

There had been meetings. More than once
Ruth had taken the podium, enjoining those
as felt aggrieved in common cause—

a long swell of oncoming waves
stiffening to granite ere it broke.
For nobody should moil
just to add wealth to those already rich!

--

Yes, at last the landscape is all mountains, said Elinor,
among tangled sweetbriers of the steep.

> Whiteface set the flint horizon
> till sometimes his own semblance

seemed to lose itself in shifting light and shadow.

> Clouds wrapped Whiteface, weather-beaten,
> thunder-scarred, wove for him
> softest fleece of gold and red.

Now hid and now revealed his lofty slopes
> did Whiteface.

> > He drew them unto himself.

Girls, does he not beckon?
with sudden longing Elinor exclaimed.

> > *Shall we not follow?*

Elinor Salutes Whiteface

*I scarce can call these peaks by common names,
they're so like human beings, not dull earth.
That entire mountain range is now fine-
woven, dyed into the texture of my mind.*

Flushed to rosy purple through soft gray,
foothills delayed withdrawing into blackness
as if they heard the voice of Elinor
and would reply. The gentle girl spoke on:

*I shan't have one memory of pain,
my shuttle flies so beautifully.
The colors of the far hills come and go,
and standing at my loom I shall behold*

*Whiteface, standing a full head taller
than his sons. A shape Titanic is he
in swathing of shroud-like pallor
sliding like a winding sheet*

*from his forehead to his feet. Once,
we watched him from the Sandwich
upland fields. Time seemed a sterile plain
till such kin brought us back to life.*

Prelude to a Ballad

> *Elinor, Bella's sick*

in the next house, Ruth volunteered. *I overheard the girls*

talking about her, saying
        that Bella mopes
much as the swollen river lay unshaped

        and vague on Sunday.

She will not eat, nor tell them how she ails.

        Go and look after her.
           Or better
        bring Bella to me, Ruth,
        as I must make haste to soothe her.

--

You girls are like a whirlwind, smiled Elinor.

In the red dawn, drowsy, you awake
from dreams to labor. At the stroke of five,

all laggards see the gates against them swing.
The stilled mills—more lake than river now.

But means to an end our labor is, to put

    fancies in a garden builded-in
    behind great walls of duty. Our true work
    is this something else.

        And Elinor took

        a certain volume
        from the hanging-shelf,

a strange medley-book

        of prose and rhyme

cut from old magazines, or pages dim
        of yellowed journals
and pasted in against the fading ink
of an old log-book

        relic of the sea.

The first tale was too long, too hard! A saga!
Read something else, begged Bella.

A song, a romance, anything.

Said Elinor, *here is a ballad of witchcraft time.*
You need not strain to hear it; let ole Peggy Bligh

        croon you off to sleep.

The Ballad of Peggy Bligh

*These days you may take the railway at will
from Halibut Point to Beacon Hill,
by Gloucester Harbor and Beverly Beach,
Salem's old steeples, Nahant's long reach.
The peek-a-boo sea companioning you.*

*But in the time of witchcraft it was not so.
If ever for Boston a ship set sail,
all secured passage—man, woman, dog—
who had errands to run in the three-hilled town.*

*Thus, one breezy midsummer morn,
Skipper Nash, of the schooner Fawn
prepared to unmoor with a crowded deck,
though a nameless terror within him roiled.*

*Taking the pulse of the crowd from the plank,
Peg's heartstrings jangled, her nerves, they twitched.
She gripped her ticket in a claw-like fist.
And the voyagers whispered 'round her name,
all a-flutter as on board she stepped.*

*From under her scarlet hood peeped an eye.
Ach! like a smoldering coal was Ole Peg's orb.
Not a soul held the crone's sharp glance*

that courted the looks it quick rebuffed.

What kind of woman would become a witch?
asked Bella. And why bother paying passage?

Variety perhaps, said Elinor.

She grew lonely, though a witch,
now that she had aged.

A fair wind wafted them down the Bay;
by noon at the Boston wharves they lay.
We shall head home at five! the skipper cried;
save Peggy, all knew well he lied.

Errands done, and anchor weighed,
out of the harbor slipped the Fawn.
But who flew down to the dock too late,
cloak a-flappin' and eye ablaze?

And on the spot, one muttered, he's rash!
As good a right had Peg, another intoned
as a monstrous gull bore down on Nash,
a red strip dangling from beak and claw.

The voyagers shrank with fear
to see that wild creature a-swoop so near.
Once, it flapped in the skipper's face,
its sharp eye glinting with a steel-cold shine.

*Once, it landed on the schooner's mast—
that blasted tree, that lichened nest—
a figurehead in a vapor-rift, silence
and the weight of loneliness binding it there.*

*Aye, it was a night more ghostly than heavenly.
The skipper daren't stir till break of day.
Then glad on the clear wave sped the Fawn.
The gull gave a cry, and flapped on its way.*

> Can't all rents be mended? Bella mused,
> like altering a gown?

>> Elinor lifted her eyes
>> from the faded ink.

> Not of souls, my dear, but let's read on.

*As they hove in sight of Salem town,
who sat on a stool by the hut on the bluff,
milking her cow with indifferent mien,
the Misery Islands just offshore?*

*Who but the witch-woman, Ole Peg Bligh!
How she got there no mortal could tell
(Psst! you might ask the gull)
for she hadn't set foot on deck or hull.*

*Well, the story goes on to say,
that Skipper Nash always rued that day*

for he lost the Fawn, and his children died,
and his wife and his cattle, and his sheep besides.

And how did Peg fare in that hut on the bluff?
When the thoughts of men took a weirder shape
than any mist that hangs round the Cape.
Before birds-of-paradise were caged in chintz
and told to make the best of it…

Bella stirred, brushed back a fawn-colored wing of hair.

Oh Elinor, I've had the strangest dreams.

As Elinor ceased, saying—
Is it a woman's fault to learn a different craft?

Ralph and Elinor

Ralph had travelled from the east
chasing the sun's smoldering ember-glow.
Bella was lost, and Ralph heeded the call,
imbibing freshness of unimagined distances.

Ralph and Elinor first said good morning
as the carriage was skirting the Androscoggin,
Elinor, a flower of delicate birth and saintly pure.
Statuesque, with such a sad back story.

They found common ground under Moat Mount's
shadow, jostled together on the horsehair seats, past
the discreet brown sides of hedges.
And like well-met streams, they braided

oak-barren sands, from Conway peaks to unsullied
lakes among gigantic mountain majesties—
becoming stone, clod, blood, damask.
They toasted happenstance as laughter rose.

Lost Girl Bella

Bright bonnets chilled Elinor with a hint
of likeness to lost Bella's. Each swam
into view, only to reveal its distinct ribbons.

Elinor had borne Bella's wearied heart
too long, sensed it wail like a babe a nurse sets down.
Add to this battling her own sense of stupor,
for the dark secret of straying still bewildered her:

how could a sister's will falter, after kindling
such a steady flame in hers?

The mystery of Death
had approached Elinor in her earliest years,
its decay hoping to siphon a flower.

Oh, Womanhood, she murmured aloud.
This is the first Death!

--

Each waking hour, Elinor spent searching
for signs of Bella in hotel books and stage offices,
undaunted by coarse looks or muttered sneers.

Daily her heart grew humbler.

Doorways poisoned her with their stench
of unclean souls, like whitened spoor
against sodden wood.

Oh, what a relief after a day like this
her room became. To snatch an hour of sleep
from the implosion of a cough.

*We go to see what we have wrought. Body,
you shall get to rest after this, lovingly shrouded.*

Elinor counted twinkling lights that went and came,
blooming and fading out like scattered poppies
dotting the sky's garden.

--

Miss, if you please, a boy said,
in tones respectful reaching out to her
a slip of paper. Word of Bella?
Good news! No more, in handwriting unknown,
and an address.

The cloak of a single page shielded her dear girl
from earth's harm!

That evening, Ralph and Elinor awaited
the last coach with anxious eagerness. Bella
stepped out, mischievous face grown paler.

With words of joy broken by sobbing questions,
Elinor caught her darling's hand.

Elinor, control yourself, Bella
said gently. Strange that such reproof
Elinor, the staid sedate, should need.

Elinor trembled. She felt her will returning
like blood to a cheek.

An unbidden thought, *I will surely die*, took hold.
Souls of her dead mother, teachers, sisters, nested
in that starry hush.

Bella's Song: When Wings are Gone

Feet must walk when wings are gone.
Lost, the cup's aroma.
Touched only now the latch. Sit here,
where you can see the treetops and the sky.

A step on the stair
filled my atmosphere.
Owning it folly, I can speak of it.
So many yards of sheeny blue, all mine!

All that freshens and uplifts
sways the thought, permits the deed
yours has but foreshadowed.

Living with a silence
can you do without me?
Did I love a phantom
in the firmament so vast?

Faded out the vision.
Will autumn be as dear?
And without you I live on,
wedded to grave duty.

On the gray horizon

*cloud-life spreads its wings
as a missing presence
stirs the woodland with a sigh.
Think me there. I am.*

Encore: Pathos of the City Lights

for Lucy Larcom

Night has hid the street, with all its motley sights,
tremulous with pathos of a half-told tale.

Strike the match, Lucy, with its thin coat of vinyl,
painted livid. Flame that lit untrodden wilderness.

But there's no chit chat—merely the whip-poor-will
en route with her companions.

Home-stars, dear guides, are glistening to life.
They tie a ribbon with her surname to a child's right wrist.

They're worried about her mouth, which is not
entirely satisfactory.

The remote, strange splendor, the familiar glow.
Night really must be setting out, though she's not a boat.

Mingle, heaven and earth! Hope flickers, burning
low and pale. Broken rays shall be loomed whole.

Queen-pioneer, who lately left our side for the vast Beyond
of Life. Tell us the unbroken story.

Robert McNamara

To Hell and Back
Including Notable Stops Along the Way

&

My SARS-CoV-2, Thus Far

Contents

To Hell and Back 41

My SARS-CoV-2, Thus Far 61

To Hell and Back
Including Notable Stops Along the Way

In a Dark Wood

Canto 1. Dante, meet Virgil.

A routine test that leaves your colon cut.
Soon your vital signs induce a fear
not felt since that Calcutta vacant lot
when a pack of furious foaming dogs appeared.

Instinctively, I stood my ground and raised
my torn umbrella like a sword and swung--
it flew apart and scattered them like jays.
My heartbeat was a hummingbird's blurred wings.

Love will not reblow life's bubble, sheen.
The signs and sine waves tell the tale. The sketch
in pen across your belly to be opened up—

what can we think but to survive. A meanness
rises in me, and I feel it catch—
I'll read. It's Dante, risen to the top.

In the Place of Lukewarm Souls
 Canto 3. Those who lived for themselves.

They chase the new, certain it is good
for them, esential proof of having lived.
And now they're chasing here, these barely dead.
Familiar faces some will mourn and love.

Their thinking off the rack, it suited the time,
was good enough, was certified as flame-
proof. Seeking pleasure overtime,
growing flaccid in comfort. Who is to blame

or praise? Just logos and the latest build,
critique compounded to surpass critique;
the over-praised, practicing low hurdles,
imagining they've climbed McKinley's peak.

I'm like them when I've asked of what I've done
only that it be interesting or fun.

Paolo and Francesca

Canto 5. Unrepented lust.

We smile for all these tumbling in love's gale
And this couple stopped to say why they are here.
For her to say, *In a garden*, they read a tale
of Lancelot and Lady Guinevere

until at last those nobles kissed. Then read
no more! *Surely, we were not to blame—*
she cries, *if only we could speak of Love to God!*
Dante swoons, thinking of tales he's rhymed.

Her careless love is phoenix-like, consumes
her lover and herself, then is reborn
betraying her husband, his brother, dumb to shame.
As one who'd been betrayed, learned self-scorn,

I wished a betrayer dead. Or so I said.
Dumb lust. Dumb luck. Why did I lose my head?

Money Money Money Money
   Canto 7. Hoarding and splurging

Frugality's the reason why we're rich,
you say, when I contest some budget buy.
And why I feel so poor, I answer, itching
merely for things of decent quality.

Here pikers and prodigals in a contradance
are chesting around a track to crash large stones.
They turn, and chest, and crash again. Comeuppance
for the obverse and the reverse of a coin.

The contradancers have no names or faces.
Undiscerning in life, they're undiscerned,
those tight-fisted, these who spent their hair,

who never could acquire a day like this—
the sky a Dodger blue, where trees that burn
in glorious dying praise autumnal airs.

Fathers and Sons (1)

Canto 10. Among the heretics.

On a soccer field for children's leagues I've seen
invasive fathers warned by posted signs:
it's not the World Cup, it doesn't matter who wins,

the coaches and referees are volunteers.
Be grateful. Everyone gets to play. Don't jeer.
Who are those fathers? Read Dante if you'd hear

of one believing that his son's fine words
would breathe eternal life into their name.
He's here because his dream was a two-edged sword—
it denied the Son resurrected and death tamed.

We only want the best for them, we tell
ourselves, when we ourselves are lacking scope
or art, to live through them when they do well--
denying death our transitory hope.

Predation 101

Canto 11: The orders of virtue

Each day I get a call to offer me
something we need to provide your in-home care.
Or an assessment, *the first hour is free.*
Exhausted, I pick up the paper, stare

at cons and madness. Is reason used for good,
or rationality to guide the will?
Is happiness ever moderately pursued?
Where among the CEOs and shills,

grifters, pimps and hustlers, prognosticators,
ad men, con men, Manafort and Flynn,
Barr and Giuliani, Pompeo, traitors,
willing to lie faithfully for gain--

Unreal, I think. What's real? You're weak with pain.
This our drought. We need no more than rain.

Remembering T. C.

Canto 13. The circle of the suicides.

He'd stolen from his father ample tranks
to quell the vicious turmoil of his brain.
Reason my go-to mode, I couldn't think
except that reason always lost to pain.

Was dumb. I said I'd miss him. What was that?
Could that pain be made into a lesson
to teach me as a friend to speak my heart?
I hope and think he felt at least its presence.

He flew to Florida *for one last fling*,
bought a companionable whore and fucked
on quiet beaches till his fair skin burned.

An animal reboot: up from a thing
abused, he slowly raised himself through muck
and needs to find again a soul that yearned.

Students and Teachers
> *Canto 15: Ser Brunetto Latini. Sodomites.*

Surprised the other's here, they speak of art
gladly relieving the teacher's pain as fiery
flecks fall on his naked skin like flaming darts.
Dante's path beside him is safely higher.

Dante had surpassed Latini's success,
that eternal life they both thought fame imparts.
He pays his debt with gratitude and praise—
for years of instruction, surrogate fathering,

even the form of epic they're speaking in—
a poet lost in a dark wood, Latini's
epic written in the vulgate Tuscan.
Teachers, we ask, what's Ser Brunetto's done?

Good students: God punishes his soul for sin.
Dante, his great student, adores the man.

Ut Pictura Poesis:

Canto 17. The Scrovegni Chapel. Usury.

We visit the chapel built by a son to appease
God's anger at his father's usury—
his metal reproducing like apple trees.
Controlled its temperature and humidity

for Giotto's lives of Jesus and his mother
in painted scenes secular as our poem—
a world of stuff, no mere symbolic ether,
with shadows from each figure's mass and volume.

The costly ultramarine has faded most—
brilliant at first, by contract painted *secco*,
never dulled uniting with the plaster.
A fine veneer, until it chipped and flaked.

Heaven was brilliant in the present tense.
We see self-glory faded to denim since.

Haruspicate or Scry

    Canto 20: The circle of fortune-tellers and diviners.

I drew uneven straws for hexagrams,
parsed dreams, my natal chart, and Tarot cards.
That boy I was is stranger to the man.
I thought to make my going forth less hard.

What did it say, that rooster pecking grain?
The birds tell all, and entrails, coffee grounds.
Economists. When will there be rain?
I shared my palms, their snaking lines and mounds,

with a true believer, sweet his every word,
post-*pranzo* in the Tuscan countryside.
Could I believe the yarrow stalks I picked

were Fortune's threat or promise from its book?
Forward then had seemed all quicksand Chance.
I wriggled forward in a blind advance.

The Art of the Deal
Canto 21: The chasm of grafters.

It's business as usual, aka graft
late-stage and crony capitalism the same
corruption of markets, judgments, honest craft,
just as favorite horses show up lame.

Examples? One or two, as Dante does—
those Catholic and Aztec sacred sites
ruined by permits to build more Walmart stores
bought from bureaucrats of the Mexican state.

And Venice bribed to let the cruise ships prance
their high-horse engines down the Grand Canal.
Old bricks corrupt and fail. Bought influence
will make of the lagoon a ruined pool.

Wake leads on to wake. In the chasm's pitch
here's Trump bribing himself, that sonofabitch.

Anger Therapy

    Canto 22: Grafters, again.

I must confess I'm big on *schadenfreude*,
watch these devils with their forks and claws
lay into grafters—what else is it but good
to fork them as they rise with open maws.

The things they never earned left cupboards bare
for those who thought that merit governed school
admissions, jobs, and contracts. A world that's fair
corrupted by their dealings, blindly cruel.

Yet Dante's devils are comic, witless in wrath.
Here two connive, are conned by a clever grafter
who flees—they fight and fall into the bath
of bubbling tar, crisped before and after.

Daily imagined murders, I hear some say,
will keep the psychotherapist away.

Welfare

    Canto 23. Hypocrites.

An administrator's discourse, smooth as snails
in tailored suit and tie. He praises work
and teachers, blandly. Pauses. Smiles.
A balanced budget hangs inside the smoke,

a budget that will break the teachers' backs.
Like smoke that's lined with bullets for the poor,
the family values on their sleeves a joke.
Feed the children, really? Here's what's more—

it isn't poverty breaks families up,
he says, but charity ruins character.
The poor might learn from him the polished step
into money left him by an ancestor

from empires built on public infrastructure.
Their heroes are the lords of the Enclosures.

Original Sin

Canto 24. Thieves

I didn't *Steal This Book*, despite the ask.
Others, yes, *Das Kapital* for one,
hidden behind my cardboard Yippie mask—
there was no *yours* and *mine*. Property was done.

I nicked the books like Augustine the pears
he shook from a neighbor's tree for love of wrong.
To make a good impression on his peers,
the way of boys in childish tough-guy songs.

And having done that, what did I do next?
Read the noble works that I now owned?
The charm of it wore off and I felt vexed,
more stupid as I tried to double down.

I understood original sin in this:
the hope of infinite and disobedient bliss.

Big Data

Canto 27. More Thieves.

My namesake, though he's surely not my double,
a 50s quant who made his name in war
mustering data to end the costly trouble
of finding parts, which ones, and where in store.

One of the whiz kids, he went on to Ford,
Henry the Second bumbling, incompetent.
He brought production units to accord.
Data was McNamara's sacrament.

Then on to the Department of Defense
with body counts to measure the Cong's attrition.
He never imagined the counts inflated, hence
his thesis was false. The generals failed their mission.

Every day Big Data's a bigger God.
The boy-kings of the Valley? Fucking odd.

Good, Clean Fun

Canto 30. One counterfeiter, one false witness.

We've got the garden up, news knocks us down.
Our undeserving president's in town,

chest-thumping like a wrestler, moves all fake.
They love this shit (who's *they*?). We feel a quake—

will it tip his cabinet of thieves and fools?
(One rides his horse to work, another drools.)

We read Hell's altercation for relief—
one liar, one fraudster, little cause for grief—

join grappling, punching, leaving their noses
more out of joint, exsanguinating roses.

Elsewhere, more are bloodied, broken, lame.
We think our pleasures, Dante, are the same

till Virgil wrecks our fun for what it is.
We're not ashamed as you for liking this.

Xaire Ezra Pound

> *Canto 31. Traitors. With lines
> from the Pisan Cantos.*

On the mountain of his work I went to school,
zigzagged Venice by foot and vaporetto
to find remaining things that he loved well.
The Quisling poet who was my Ser Brunetto,

up to his chin in a lake of ice. I go
toward him and his traitor heroes, his shout out:
*Xaire Alessandro, Xaire Fernando
e il Capo, Pierre, Vidkun, Henriot—*

that's Mussolini hanging upside down,
two Vichy politicians, one tried and shot,
one the Resistance killed, like Pound
a radio propagandist and a poet.

What was it he loved well? Beauty wedded
to economics. A match made in hell.

Fathers and Sons (2)

Canto 33. Count Ugolino and Archbishop Ruggieri.

He knows revenge a dish that's best served cold
and so he grimly gnaws the frozen head
of his betrayer. Strangely we aren't told
why he is here—it can't be just to feed.

His tale begs pity, treated so unfair,
incarcerated without water, food,
with his young sons to watch each one expire.
He tells his every feeling, every mood.

Of comfort for his boys, no words he gave.
They saw him gnaw his hand. They offered him
their flesh to save his life. He felt their love
more pain. No pity for them. We ache for them,

the loving creatures of a treasonous dad,
who died uncomforted for what he did.

Ends Well

Canto 34. Climbing over Satan.

Our last half-year's been strenuous as hell,
it shook the ground we stand on to its core.
You'll die, you'll live, but never will be well.
At best, on dark nights, promise in the stars.

A little hell. Surprised we flourished there?
We're nothing special, surely *that* we know.
How many friends are tried with harder fare.
(Comparisons are heartless, best let go,

of no importance on the scale of death
that weighs us with its creaky rusting springs.)
And though we squabble over trivial things

when Death with chessboard came, we saved our breath
for final things, beloved, in our life—
and Dante never writes about his wife.

My SARS-CoV-2, Thus Far

The dead lay in the streets, a nauseous stench—
Defoe of London, Boccaccio of Florence.
Night carts clatter, Ubering the dead.

Masked and gloved, I walk my neighborhood—
spring snow pinking the cherry trees,
and houses, their oddities, small victories

of architecture and garden. First petals fall.
Buttressing routines begin to fail.
The president receives an invitation

to offer words of comfort to the nation.
He spits it back: *That's a nasty question.*
He leaves the briefing, scowl intact.

*

They comforted their mother in the waiting room, then asked outside an exam room when they could see their mother again. The sign on the door said, *no entrance without protective equipment*, and the nurse, *not until she's ready to come home.*

I sat on a gurney in the hallway because the rooms were full, because I'd sliced my hand while sharpening a knife. An intern stitched me up, while next to me they asked, *What should we do?* The nurse's answer, *Go home and stay there.*

Soon we'd all be staying home. One evening on *Nature*, I watched a cheetah's little shuffle step shiver the grass before it leapt on a springbok that missed or misread the sign of danger. What signs did we misread, ignore, to be caught so unprepared? The predator eats by rote—the thighs, the ribs, etcetera, until the offal sits on bones full of fatty marrow, rich as croissants.

The easy mistake. The ziggurat of bones.

*

The chalk-white lines on a neighbor's roof
are prisoners' scratches, proof

like a beard of our time done inside
with an hour a day for exercise.

They're poison for the clots of moss.
Hydroxychloroquine, says the Boss,

is poison for the coronavirus!
The huckster tires us.

A Texas politician cries,
let the old give up their lives

a sacrifice for daughters and sons,
to feed an economy about to swoon.

Preaching with great sincerity
the Gospel of Prosperity.

*

Wash and disinfect and wash again. All we love
made sterile, though not by a Midas touch.

On 16th Street, the cherry trees' last blooms take refuge in niches of new leaves. Light catches them out, brilliant in day's gloom. The trees are for this alone, not fruit.

At senior hour, we walk to Trader Joe's, *hello* to all those we avoid. *Six feet apart not six feet under*, says a poster. Does the idiom translate? I wonder. Is anyone left who puts their dead in trees?

My mother, incinerated, on the mantelpiece.

*

For exercise we walk
two miles to a rock

called the Wedgwood erratic,
plunked down, hypnotic

glacial dropping looming large
as a single-car garage,

eroding back to earth
as we arc toward our deaths.

It asks of us our merest bare
awareness.

Harry says he wants
to paint it. Standing once

on its parking strip, he began
sketching. I heard canvas

in my mind being stretched.

*

The Times reports the virus is a pleomorphic
particle with bulbous protrusions. In illustrations,
a rubber ball studded with carmine stakes. In
electron micrographs, a jumble of grey-scale
bubbles.

Bat-bred it flew as from a shook cape. We'd seen
it coming, or some had, in the flicker before
denial. Nothing, really. They did nothing.

Crows in a murder hector an eagle until it flies
off, then gather around a dead cat on the road,
their urban staging. Hector never wasted time

hectoring, too busy wrestling with his courage.
The crows are boisterous, bullying, strutting,
presidential, a cowardice corseted for TV.

*

Starting the day in slacks, a collared shirt, a tweed
vest, alters how I read

the ornamental pear in bloom this ill
season. A tree some call

a junk tree—ragged of architecture,
in a hard breeze unsure.

The meaning has no meaning but to dress,
helpless otherwise, in distress.

*

Medicine. A sorrow and a crisis, a puzzle practical
and theoretical. Like acute respiratory distress,
but different. Some asked what cause, others
how to ease the breathing. Then it wasn't the
lungs alone, but kidney failure, stroke, heart
attack, blood clotting in every organ, even in

dialysis tubes. Endothelial injury and
dysregulation? What cause and what treatment.

Politics. A shortage of PPE the doctors and nurses
needed, caused in part by hoarding. Mostly,
though, by Trump and Pompeo selling tons of it to
China, because hey, we'd never need it.

Economics. Also without PPE, the workers in
supermarkets and pharmacies and warehouses, in
meat-packing plants and delivery services, many
who work for unliving wages without insurance,
who work endangered, so the rest of us will get
food and the medicines we need. (People too
small to be sung, I give you this simple verse.)

To the roof-top man with a broom removing
moss that tumbles living to the ground,
blessings!
To the radishes and peas erupting, the
chickadees nesting, the robins in the outfield
grass, looking from mound to bull pen, good
luck! I wait with you!
And to sky unclouded, to our shadows and the
welcome shade, to the air so sweet and clear on
the horizon, blessings on you, our silver lining!

Neighbors, I wave to you with hands well-washed and disinfected, what connects us and distances, frightens and reassures.

*

If God rested on the seventh day, Creation would have collapsed, like *that*. A creator creates from himself, out of himself, the whole magnificent terrifying edifice, living and changing. What could sustain it but the Creator, those rabbis asked, His being the being of the world.

Unlike the Pazzi Chapel without Brunelleschi, the variations on Mont Sainte-Victoire without Cezanne. They were re-arrangers of matter into forms they themselves did not create but received, like the forms of spirit that lift us from our wallowing in desire, for this—no, that, *ad infinitum*. No sooner had than lost.

Trophies and brass rings, certificates and raises, who will love us? Whose love is that strong? On the Sabbath, at least, give it a rest.

*

I've failed you, you agree, not having stayed
six feet away with your mask always
in place. And then, who we said we'd allow
into the house. Life's complex as the oral law

born of centuries of rabbinic debate.
And though you carefully disinfected plates
and every surface that he might have touched
as you helped him set up tech to keep in touch,

to prefer the real to paranoid delusions
such as drove him from home, confusion,
a racket in the street surely a mob
coming after him for a bungled job—

the no-offense grown a boulder.
God was at your motherly shoulder
in huddled closeness, unmasking for a beer
and snacks. I kept myself apart, in fear—

being old and compromised. Distressed
as always, your son, and you who he trusts.
Later we spoke of the good
of distancing and masks, however hard.

Then asked, what could it mean to fail,
risking for him, a risk how large or small,
something done as foolish as love is
at times, the good of being risked as well.

*

His yellow jacket circumambulates his house.
The path, I'm told, leads past two bowls of
stones. He takes from one, walks to the other,
gives, counting what's done and what's to do.
Three months ago we'd walk in the park, stop at
some cafe to chew the fat. I think of Molloy and
his sucking stones, the problem of right order in
social arrangements. These days nothing is more
clear.

Clanging pots of pseudo-rights and guns demand
an end to public health. Be courageous, they say,
ready to risk the lives of others, their families and
parents, their friends and fellow parish members.
Fine, we'll let the city open. Who will go to bars
and restaurants and theaters or their bathrooms?
Six feet apart is still too close to loud spit talkers.

We'll be back in public when vaccinated. At
night there's opera streaming on TV, chamber
music and the international cop shows we
devour. We walk around the neighborhood each
day, enjoy our conversation. No bar is worth an
agonizing death.

You think the virus is a hoax?
Hydroxychloroquine, injected light and Clorox,
the deep state? My question marks are done.
Anything, everywhere. Amen.

*

A dry season.
The poppies are full blown
in floppy gossamer and flame.

I find my amplitude in my solitude.
An old man staying home.

Erin M. Bertram

Gender/Genre

We get this body and we get choices.
—Arianne Zwartjes

*If we want to think about genre like gender
it means we are thinking of
the book as body.*
—Kazim Ali

Maybe a clue to my existence is being en route, liminal, occupying a third space. In between Xs on the map. Say, in the car—driving, or a passenger, or sitting at a gas station while my wife is using the restroom or buying a coke. My mother says that when I was little & couldn't sleep, she, all sleep-clogged & groggy, would strap my small body into the car seat & drive off into the night, morning breath already forming, sleep wedged in our tired, hazy eyes. She'd drive like that, while I slept next to her. She'd drive & drive while I slept, for the both of us, wrapped in my pink-checked, satin-rimmed baby blanket, exhaling soft, wet baby sighs.

When I imagine this—when I remember it?—which I do, often, the car smells of summer nights & ashtrays & promise, whatever that smells like. The car, in which, a few years later, I'd store my rock collection, is laced with equal parts exhaustion & love. Her own mother had died only a few months earlier—wrecked by cancer, rendered someone else entirely, having disowned my mother a few days before her wedding day, discarding most of her belongings in a single blind hot fit.

What was my mother thinking on those endless nights, tracing the same quiet roads to sleep? Did she resent me for making her get behind the wheel like that? How does she feel now when she remembers glancing over at me, lying there, asleep, catching, for a moment, my quiet girl face, so trusting & still, in the cool wash of a sudden streetlight?

Several summers ago, my mother & I rode a half-ton of horse across a small fork of river in the Sonora Desert that we never thought to look up on a map. The guide was stoic, had us crushing sage between our palms to release the smoky fragrance. My aunt waited for us back at the corral; a horse, startled, had nearly crushed her leg, decades earlier, when it lost its footing. I remember the sunburn, the flies, the water rushing over the horse's doorknob knees. I'd ridden before, but I was awe-struck, noodle-legged, blinking unbelief & muscle ache the next morning.

My mother, on the other hand, rode quietly behind me, snapping photos of the two of us, steady as a glass of water resting on the horse's wide back. In one photo, all you can see is my body, just bust & four limbs, the chestnut horse, & the curves of a mesquite tree, my breasts massive in the high noon sun. I love the photo for its grit, its out-of-focus reality. But my body, ample in the desert heat, leaves something unsaid.

Often I wish I could remove them, simply unlatch the rusted hinges & hang them on the wall, the way I would a ball cap or coat after a long day. Just hang them on the wall & walk away. Never look back.

My breasts are beautiful. Stunning, really. They just don't belong on my body.

Downtown, just before the New Year, we all made mini figures of ourselves at a toy store. I made two

Erins that night: one with sideburns & one without. The one with looks happier—pocketed then, later hidden, bedside.

Later, when I looked up gender in the dictionary, I found this at the bottom of the page:

OTHER PSYCHOLOGY TERMS: fetish, hypochondria, intelligence, mania, narcissism, neurosis, pathological, psychosis, schadenfreude, subliminal

Given my search term, what possible positives could have emerged as a result of this juxtaposition?

In other words, why does this list exist at all?

———————

The body wants what it wants. Isn't that true? Isn't that how the story goes? *Close your eyes—picture the look of me kissing your quiet eyes.*

She is a rocky shore of smooth, fist-sized stones where salt laps at the land. Or is she fire instead, lit from within, me staring dumbstruck at the low glow. What embers remain when the campfire of the body dies out? Thunder. Lightning. A tarpaulin calm draping everything with rain.

What hot coals hiss as the sky breaks open upon them?

On more than one occasion, I've come home from work with so much to say, but not all the words, so it amounts to nothing. Or almost nothing. But everything that's real casts a shadow, doesn't it? There have been flies in my kitchen, quietly feasting on the soft flesh of bananas, peaches, the translucent liquid beans are canned in. Heat lightning. The white noise of the refrigerator. A sky so bewilderingly deep that, on looking up, you're liable to lose your footing.

Many summers ago, I nearly drowned on a rafting trip in a river whose name translates to "River of Lost Souls." I remember looking up through feet of backlit emerald water milky with sediment & current. I was alone. It was beautiful, so quiet. I thought I was going to die. When I surfaced, it was as if my life had just happened without me.

Years earlier, in high school, I'd wanted a classmate's hands on me like sunburn, like water rushing over me the way the current draws its fingers, lightly, repeatedly, over river stones, burnishing, rendering them, in time, changed, slowly softened by her touch.

When categorizing American bison, some biologists have referred to them in threes: northern plains bison, woods bison, & southern plains bison. These megafauna used to roam the grasslands in herds, walking many miles a day & braying under the noon sun, & bedding down together for coverage amid spindrift & high winds.

Their migration paths toward feeding grounds, watering holes, & salt licks, guided by nothing but instinct, lessened the burden for innumerable pioneers after them.

So many giant hooves pounding a path toward the ocean.

That time at the coffee shop, when the Women's room was locked, so I used the Men's instead & got my period. The whole day, the whole week afterward, I couldn't forget how the body—*my* body—insists on itself despite me.

And that time after math class, sixth grade, when my teacher got up to draw something on the board—something I didn't understand—& I bled through my pants onto the chair. I remember feeling ashamed, not for what I'd done, but for what had happened to me.

How the body, in this way, could be said to betray.

How the body's wildernesses refuse to be fenced in.

It's most acute when I'm in the shower, the lather fragrant with mint or sea salt, eucalyptus, vetiver, rose rounding the curves of my body, my breasts two dumb weights hanging either side of my heart.

When I get dressed, when I remove my clothes, the pink marks between neck & shoulder are proof of the tension, proof that a part of myself has never really felt part of me at all.

And when I'm in bed with my wife, moving together like we do, my boxer briefs left on, necessary, my chest, even beneath the taught elastane, swaying like strange water. I'm a neoprene diver aiming steadily at the surface.

We don't touch them, really. Trained ourselves not to. We've trained our attention elsewhere.

I can't help but think of my grandmother, decades ago, soaking, by candlelight, in a hot claw-foot tub, the bathroom door latched, Epsom salts & camphor. Her arms crossed to cover the scars, ashamed for her young children, my mother & aunt, to see what the doctors had to do to her in order to save her life.

The urge to believe is stronger than belief itself.

Back when I taught college, a student of mine wrote about roller derby, bipolar, possibly being bisexual, & Derrida's concept of *différance*. Only after re-reading her essay for the third time, late at night when I can't sleep, does it dawn on me that the look of my name (Erin) vs. the sound of my name (// Aaron) is a prime example of *différance*.

Within a binary system, one component tends to differ.

Within a binary system, one component tends to defer to the other.

While the written may be prized over the spoken, I hold the dual iterations of my name close to my chest, warm & breathing.

As a child, I got visibly upset when my mother called me *pretty*, could tell I confused her by the look on her face every time. Was the man when my friends & I played dress-up, though I didn't know what that meant, only that I didn't want to be the other thing, sneaking my dad's old cowboy boots, his blazers & ties, dancing to "Uptown Girl." Knowing I was doing something wrong &, for once, doing it anyway.

Sometimes a girl friend & I would pretend we were having sex & I didn't know who was the boy, but we never touched, not that way. We'd lay on her twin bed, she behind me, pressed against me & holding me close, & we'd move together like that in the daylight, not making any sound, hoping her mother wouldn't walk in & find us that way, together.

Sometimes, during recess, a girl friend & I secretly shaped sand castles of a naked lady laying down, in the long jump pit out past the playground. Though, each time, when the bell rang, we'd kill the lady, fumble to hide the evidence, then line up in girl-rows & boy-rows—a concept, even then, I never understood—& head, quietly, back to our seats.

The relief was immediate, vast, uncontrollable, when, a few years ago, my brother asked me to stand in his wedding, said I could wear a tuxedo instead of a bridesmaids dress—the pink, the strapless, the tulle.

My breath came easier. I didn't have to worry. Not as much.

I didn't have the money to send the jacket out for proper alterations, to a place where they make what's meant for a man for someone else instead, so I didn't fill the shoulders & my chest was broad in ways the cloth didn't forgive. In the photographs, though—I note the change—I hold my head high. In the photographs, I'm smiling.

There are cisgender bodies & transgender bodies—*trans-* from the Latin for "across," *cis-* for "on this side of." But what of the bodies pitched partway between, in the valley bordered by adjacent, towering peaks—the gravel, perhaps, sloped more steeply on one side? What is this land called? Could this be *woman*, too?

A dream: I'm walking, alone, down a dirt road carrying a bag—not too heavy, but I feel its weight press the small of my back—the sun as it usually is in summer, foliage lush, the sweetness of bloom & damp rot pungent on all sides. A trio of kids plays war at the side of the road. I overhear them talking about me. The loudest asks *Are you a boy or a girl?*

I reply, coolly as I can, *What do you think?*, no trace of malice in my voice, only curiosity. We have a conversation I don't remember. As I walk away, as if in epilogue, someone says *I think you're a girl, but you don't care*. Who said it, I can't be sure. But they were right.

And yet the occasional stall at the end of the hall—a tiny room with no windows, a mirror above the sink, light reflecting off the cool clean surfaces, & a door that locks behind me.

Only one way in & only one way out. A welcome surprise, this beam of austere clarity.

On the door hangs a sign, sometimes plastic, sometimes bearing the smudges of printer ink, often with a line drawn neatly down the middle: *He?* on the left, *She?* on the right. And me, standing straight, stiff as a board, standing upright, leaned slightly to one side, between them.

I cut my hair short because it was 100 degrees nearly every day that summer. Because my wife owns electronic clippers, an indulgence I could never justify for myself. I did it just before my mother & aunt visited for the weekend from Illinois. What I didn't realize, as my then-fiancé pressed the shiny metal to my skin, was that my cropped hair would remind them of their own mother, decades earlier, as she struggled to surface from chemotherapy & radiation for a tumor the size of a baby's fist lodged deep within her breast. The tumor would spread its ribbon-fingers throughout her body until, closing in on bone, lung, thyroid, memory, it took her down with it. Everything was different after that.

What I'd failed to remember, despite my own mother's single mastectomy ten years before, was that images don't disappear just because they're gone. It wasn't my un-ladylike appearance that startled my family when I picked them up from the airport that afternoon. They know me. It was that, fused with the memory of their dying mother's face—the high cheekbones; the dimpled cheeks, one side more pronounced than the other; the bookish brown eyes; the stubble-for-hair—the unmistakable softness, like down, like something that doesn't yet know what it might become. What, seemingly, it must be.

It was gender, but the wrong one. And the beloved, but not who they expected in the Great Plains heat & wind. They weren't cruel, just sad, which they tried to hide with comments & small jokes about what they saw out the window as we drove. Bright potted flowers. A few geese. I told them how sorry I was. All they could do was look back at me & be seen in their sorrow, cushion it with their small words. All I could do was laugh along.

Ironically, the considered procedure is sometimes, crudely, referred to as a *gender mastectomy*.

A misnomer, yes, & yet we understand completely.

Don't we?

I browse *Before* & *After* top surgery videos online, scroll through photo after photo, the dull blue light of the screen a beacon in these uneasy waters, wondering what color, what shape, what texture my scars will take.

What stories they'll take on. What stories they'll tell.

Will they be raised like the contours of a new tattoo, all peak & valley plain, terrain weathered, dried blood, the scab softened by time, color suspended in the spaces that remain?

Or will they, instead, be smooth & carry a light sheen, subtle, quiet, like the white cord draped across my mother's chest?

Once, after work, I walked into the Men's room & did not look back. I pulled open the heavy door & walked quickly to the nearest stall, tried locking it behind me but it wouldn't close so I tried forcing it. I closed my eyes, breathed in deeply one two three four five, then gingerly pushed the door open, noting the one-inch squares of hard bathroom floor reflecting my every move.

In the next stall over, just like the first, I pulled the door closed as if barricading myself in, my pulse driving its hard, steady beat deep into my body. I could feel it in my cheeks, my fingertips, the softness of my belly. After placing strips of toilet paper on either side of the Men's seat, I sat on the Men's toilet, struggling to breathe out without making a sound so that, if any men walked in, they'd see my Men's shoes, but they wouldn't hear my Women's exhale.

I feared for my safety, even though there were no men in the room, even though they may not have noticed or cared. Only me. Only ghost-men. What if I prefer the hot, illicit fear of the Men's room to the familiar, illicit fear of the Women's? How many more times will I be able to do this without getting caught? Without paying for it?

———————

The first time I realized gender existed, I was three, maybe four years old, though I didn't have language for it then. It was preschool. I was sitting on the giant red rug with the colorful numbers & letters on it, next to my favorite teacher, the bookmobile lady. She was holding a cornflower blue felt board onto which, every morning, sitting in a tight knee-to-knee circle, we'd answer what the weather was like that day. She'd press, to the board, a large felt sun wearing sunglasses, or a cloud wearing a frown, or a snowflake in a stocking cap, holding it out, at arm's length, for all of us to see.

I remember the slick of her short black hair. The warm sturdiness of her lady-voice. The tiny hairs on her forearms. It was preschool. I knew the weather & how to sit in a circle like good boys & girls. What I didn't know was why blushing when I got to sit next to my favorite teacher was wrong.

We were in the car, my father & me. I was ten years old. I preferred the windows, but when he turned on the air, it smelled like cool basement & steel, & I was surprised, every time, that I liked it. My knees were scraped. I had a bowl haircut; he had stubble. We were driving home from one of my soccer games, the sun so bright it hurt my eyes, & when I closed them I saw the soft red-black. My white jersey had a collar & grass stains, our last name block-lettered across my back.

He smelled like deodorant & sweat. He loves me, even though he didn't talk much. He says everything with his eyes, brown & deep & quiet like mine. I hated soccer. Hated the speed & pressure & rules of it. The push of it. The shove. And the clock, always ticking. Keeping time. Timing me. But I loved winding up & kicking the ball hard across the field—the build, the rush, the swift-sturdy movement of muscles working in unison, hard, against the wind. I hated the game, but I love him, so I played. He got yellow cards sometimes when he talked loudly, bought oranges for my team to eat at halftime, the juice everywhere, the stickiness, the glee, half-rinds discarded shells beached across the grass.

Sometimes, at home, I'd sneak into the medicine cabinet to breathe in the musk & mint & manliness of his deodorant, its heady allure, what I now recognize as notes of sandalwood & vetiver, a locked & unspoken room. I felt guilty, I did, but not enough to stop. Was I enough, or too much, of a son for him?

Reading all I can about the considered procedure, I encounter clinical language similar to what I found, a dozen years back, reading all I could about my mother's procedure:

> *The specific technique used is dependent on a patient's scar preference as well as breast size and anatomy. This procedure is done under general anesthesia and patients typically will go home the same day as an outpatient procedure.*

> *You may be discharged home with surgical drains in your breasts, which will be removed when output decreases in the first one to two weeks after surgery. You will be able to resume light activities one to two days after surgery.*

I wanted to join the Men's monthly themed subscription box club because I like the themes they offer: Savor, Concentrate, Chill, Bloom, Getaway. Each box contains a few items to facilitate a given experience, like wine-tasting, weekend travel, or a home office desk clean & functional as arithmetic.

This month it's a scrimshaw pocket-knife kit. I plan to etch & ink a bison onto it, whose migration trails carved countless paths deep into the American wilderness.

I now realize I also wanted to join the club because a box will arrive each month—a box intended for men—with my name on it.

———————

When I went "Say *Yes* to the Vest" shopping, for my wedding, with my mother & my aunt, they didn't scoff at the name I gave our department store adventure. Instead, they followed me to the Men's section, asked what size I was looking for—not in hushed tones, I noticed, suggesting they were with me, they were trying. I needed a M, maybe a L, & they held out a few vests for my approval—mostly patterned or colorful, not exactly my taste—but I tried each one on anyway.

In the Women's fitting room, which put my mother at ease, they stood outside the slatted door, waiting. They waited patiently for me to let them in. And I stood in that tiny room alone, nineteen Men's vests hanging on metal hooks on the wall.

Each time, I buttoned the vest down to my waist, leaving the final button open because of my hips. Each time, I turned around & looked myself in the eye. I saw the way the vest hung on the form that I was given.

Early on in our relationship, my wife asked if it was okay if she said I was *beautiful*. I was moved, deeply so—she felt the word described me, & she considered my relationship to it given my gender, my given & chosen genre.

She asked if I prefer *handsome* to *beautiful* a year or so later. My eyes wet with gratitude again, & I said yes, but also *either*, though we now both know my preference. Silence took over the moment. She left me balancing with the weight of a single, unbidden magic word.

She told me, then, of a writer who refers to her spouse as her *husband-wife*. Told me this with wide eyes—generous, expectant of something neither of us could define, attentive to the myriad ways that both language & gaze mark our moments. And though the word doesn't fit my body as it moves—headlong, stammering, at times easeful—through the world, I considered it over the following months, rolled it over in my palm, feeling for demarcations, erosion, the smell of salt or steel or smoke it left behind.

Notes

The epigraphs are from Arianne Zwartjes's *Detailing Trauma: A Poetic Anatomy* and Kazim Ali's "Genre-Queer: Notes Against Generic Binaries." Portions of this project were adapted from the following sources: Alix Olson's "the urge to believe is stronger than belief itself," Bespoke Post's website, the University of Wisconsin Hospitals and Clinics Authority's "Gender Mastectomy" webpage, the "Michel Foucault" entry on Theory.org.uk, and the *Merriam-Webster Dictionary*.

Biographies & Acknowledgments

Deborah Woodard is the author of *Plato's Bad Horse* (Bear Star, 2006) *Borrowed Tales* (Stockport Flats, 2012) and *No Finis: Triangle Testimonies, 1911* (Ravenna Press, 2018). She has also translated the poetry of Amelia Rosselli from Italian in *The Dragonfly, A Selection of Poems: 1953-1981* (Chelsea Editions, 2009), *Hospital Series* (New Directions, 2015) and *Obtuse Diary* (Entre Rios Books, 2018). A 2019 Pushcart Prize nominee, Deborah teaches at Hugo House in Seattle and co-curates the Belltown-based reading series Margin Shift.

Robert McNamara has published three books of poetry, most recently *Incomplete Strangers* (Lost Horse Press) and a co-translation of poems by the Bengali poet Sarat Kumar Mukhopadhyay, *The Cat Under the Stairs* (EWU Press). His poems have appeared widely in journals and anthologies, including *The Sorrow Psalms* (Iowa) and *The Book of Irish-American Poetry* (Notre Dame). He has received fellowships for writing from the National Endowment for the Arts and the Fulbright Commission, and for many years was the editor of L'Epervier Press. Retired from teaching at the University of Washington, he now lives and writes in Seattle.

Erin M. Bertram was a published finalist in the 2013 *Diagram* Hybrid Essay Contest, and her thirteenth chapbook, *Relief Map* (2017), won the Summer Tide Pool Chapbook Prize. She holds an MFA from Washington University in St. Louis, a PhD in English/Creative Writing from the University of Nebraska-Lincoln, and specializations in Women's & Gender Studies at both levels. A former college teacher of ten years, she is a Writing Coach & Consultant with One Lit Place and WriteByNight in northern Illinois. Her first book, *It's Not a Lonely World: A Memoir on the Edge* (Trembling Pillow Press, forthcoming), received the 2017 Karen Dunning Creative Activity Award.

Thank you to the editors of the following publications for giving much of this work an initial audience: *Fourteen Hills*, *South Dakota Review*, and *Tarpaulin Sky*. I'm also grateful to the University of Nebraska-Lincoln for fellowships and awards that supported the research and writing of this work.